This Little Tiger book belongs to:

For Rea (and her new home) x
- S C

For my family and good friends . . .
- C P

LITTLE TIGER PRESS
1 The Coda Centre,
189 Munster Road, London SW6 6AW
www.littletiger.co.uk
First published in Great Britain 2015
This edition published 2015
Text by Suzanne Chiew
Text copyright © Little Tiger Press 2015
Illustrations copyright © Caroline Pedler 2015

Caroline Pedler has asserted her right to be
identified as the illustrator of this work under
the Copyright, Designs and Patents Act, 1988

A CIP catalogue record for this book is available from the British Library

Printed in China • LTP/1400/1004/1114

2 4 6 8 10 9 7 5 3 1

Badger AND THE Great STORM

Suzanne Chiew • Caroline Pedler

LITTLE TIGER PRESS
London

"*Mighty oaks from acorns grow!*" sang Badger as he bustled round his cosy burrow. Tucked beneath the roots of the old oak tree, it had always been a happy home for badgers.

Suddenly, there was a squeak at the window. "Badger!" cried Mouse. "Have you heard? A terrible storm is coming!"

"A storm?" cried Rabbit, hopping up.
"My nest will blow away!" flapped Bird.
"And what about my lettuce garden?"
Hedgehog gasped. "Badger! Whatever
will we do?"

"Don't worry!" smiled Badger. "We'll
make your homes as strong as castles!"

First, Badger made a sturdy door for Rabbit's burrow. "To keep out the wild winds!" he said.

Then, he used some upturned flowerpots to cover Hedgehog's prize lettuces . . .

and built a nest box
to keep Bird safe
and dry.

"There!" sighed Badger happily, tying Mouse's ladder in place.

"Thank you, Badger!" Mouse squeaked. "Now please hurry home - the storm is nearly here!"

Badger trudged back towards his old oak tree but very soon the rain was pouring down.

"Oh dear!" Badger frowned, as thunder crashed and the wind howled. "Oh dear, oh dear!"

Suddenly a door flew open.
"Badger!" yelled Rabbit. "You
must come in from the storm!"
"It is a bit blustery!" chuckled
Badger, following Rabbit inside.

The baby bunnies gathered round.
"Will we get blown away?" they cried.
"We're quite safe here," said Badger
gently. "Now, who would like a
story?" And as they snuggled close,
the bunnies soon forgot to be
scared.

All through the night, the storm roared and raged. Thunder boomed, lightning flashed and the animals shivered in their homes, waiting for morning to arrive.

But when the sun came up,
the friends had a terrible shock.
"Where will poor Badger live now?"
gasped Hedgehog. "There have always
been badgers under that old oak tree!"

"He can stay with me,"
trilled Bird, "though
my nest is very high."

"Or with me," suggested
Mouse, "though it might
be a squeeze."

"He can share with me!" cried Hedgehog. "But we'll need a lot more leaves to snuggle beneath!"

Badger took a deep breath. "Don't worry," he said slowly. "Every problem has a solution!"

When Badger and Rabbit arrived the friends rushed over.

"My poor, poor house," Badger sighed sadly.

"How can we help?" squeaked Mouse.

"Yes, what can we do?" asked Hedgehog.

"First let's rescue my books and gather my pans," called Badger. "Then we'll turn this grand old oak into a brand new house!"

The friends set to work at once. There was a job for everyone, no matter how small.

For days and days they chopped and sawed . . .

and hammered and painted . . .

until they had used every last piece of wood to build something very special . . .

"My wonderful new home!" beamed
Badger. "You're the best friends I could
ever wish for!"

Just then, Hedgehog rushed over.
"We forgot to use this!" he cried,
holding up a tiny acorn.

"I know just what we'll do with that," said Badger. "Mighty oaks from acorns grow!"

He dug a little hole and they planted it very carefully.

And from that day on, and for ever more, there were always badgers living under the new oak tree.

More fantastic tales of fun and friendship from Little Tiger Press!

BOO!
Tracey Corderoy · Caroline Pedler

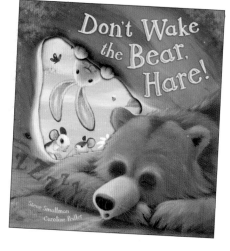

Don't Wake the Bear, Hare!
Steve Smallman · Caroline Pedler

Super-Duper Dudley!
Sue Mongredien

There's No Such Thing As MONSTERS!
Steve Smallman · Caroline Pedler

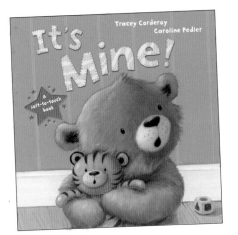

Tracey Corderoy · Caroline Pedler
It's Mine!
A soft-to-touch book

That's What Friends Are For
Julia Hubery · Caroline Pedler

For information regarding any of the above titles
or for our catalogue, please contact us:
Little Tiger Press, 1 The Coda Centre,
189 Munster Road, London SW6 6AW
Tel: 020 7385 6333
Fax: 020 7385 7333
E-mail: contact@littletiger.co.uk
www.littletiger.co.uk